HACK/SLASH™
/EVA™
VOLUME ONE
MONSTER'S BALL

HACK/SLASH

CASSIE HACK:

A 21ST CENTURY ANTI-HEROINE WHO HAS DEVOTED HER LIFE TO THE ELIMINATION OF "SLASHERS" WHO KILL WITHOUT MERCY OR REASON.

WRITTEN BY
BRANDON JERWA

ILLUSTRATED BY
CEZAR RAZEK

LETTERED BY
MARSHALL DILLON

COLORED BY
SALVATORE AIALA (ISSUES 1-3)
& INLIGHT STUDIOS (ISSUE 4)

COLLECTION COVER BY
TIM SEELEY

HACK/SLASH CREATED BY
TIM SEELEY

EVA CO-DEVELOPED BY
JIM KUHORIC

EVA™ VOLUME ONE MONSTER'S BALL

EVA:

A TIME-LOST WARRIOR WHO BELIEVES THAT GOD WANTS HER TO RID OUR WORLD OF THE FOUL THINGS THAT LURK IN THE SHADOWS.

DYNAMITE® ENTERTAINMENT

NICK BARRUCCI • PRESIDENT
JUAN COLLADO • CHIEF OPERATING OFFICER
JOSEPH RYBANDT • EDITOR
JOSH JOHNSON • CREATIVE DIRECTOR
RICH YOUNG • DIRECTOR BUSINESS DEVELOPMENT
JASON ULLMEYER • SENIOR DESIGNER
JOSH GREEN • TRAFFIC COORDINATOR
CHRIS CANIANO • PRODUCTION ASSISTANT

image®

ROBERT KIRKMAN • CHIEF OPERATING OFFICER
ERIK LARSEN • CHIEF FINANCIAL OFFICER
TODD McFARLANE • PRESIDENT
MARC SILVESTRI • CHIEF EXECUTIVE OFFICER
JIM VALENTINO • VICE-PRESIDENT

ERIC STEPHENSEN • PUBLISHER
TODD MARTINEZ • SALES & LICENSING COORDINATOR
BETSY GOMEZ • PR & MARKETING COORDINATOR
BRAWYN BIGGLESTONE • ACCOUNTS MANAGER
SARAH deLAINE • ADMINISTRATIVE ASSISTANT
TYLER SKAINLINE • PRODUCTION MANAGER
DREW GILL • ART DIRECTOR
JONATHAN CHAN • PRODUCTION ARTIST
MONICA HOWARD • PRODUCTION ARTIST
VINCENT KAKUA • PRODUCTION ARTIST
KEVIN YUEN • PRODUCTION ARTIST

ISBN-10: 1-60690-249-0 ISBN-13: 978-1-60690-249-3 First Printing 10 9 8 7 6 5 4 3 2 1

HACK/SLASH™/EVA™ VOLUME ONE: MONSTER'S BALL. First printing. Contains materials originally published in Hack/Slash/Eva: Monster's Ball #1-4. Published by Dynamite Entertainment. 155 Ninth Ave. Suite B, Runnemede, NJ 08078.
Printed in China.

Quantity Purchases: Companies, professional groups, clubs, and other organizations may qualify for special terms when ordering quantities of this title. For information, direct your inquiry to the Special Sales Department.

For media rights, foreign rights, promotions, licensing, and advertising: marketing@dynamite.net

ISSUE ONE

From the journals of
Victor Frankenstein:
In this matter of creation I have been fraught with uncertainty. It is often an absence of faith in my own ability that blinkers my eyes when I need them most, but not this day.
I have seen the shape of things to come, and it has engendered in me a sense of obsession: I must possess the Philosopher's Stone.
I'll not embarrass myself by speculating on the extent of its power; all accounts are apocryphal, and I suspect they underestimate the potential of the thing.
One thing is known. The Stone holds the link between intellectual science and arcane mysticism.
It is true that I have achieved my goal. I have created life from dead matter!
But know as I do: Flesh animated by electric breath; form given the function of impulse – it is life, but it is not alive. Not truly.
There is dimness in the eyes. A human brain reanimated commands the motion and focus of the gaze, but it cannot imbue those eyes with light.
It is the heart that makes the light; a true heart, not my simple device of fluid pumps and metronomic rhythm.
The Stone shall be the heart.

I am no rival to God. I do not aspire to usurp my creator, though many of my peers might suggest otherwise.
PROPERTY CLOSED
FOR DEVELOPMENT
TRESPASSERS WILL BE PROSECUTED
If we are servants of God's will, as the scriptures insist, who can judge me? Who can presume to know what forces guide my hand?

FRANKLIN MOTOR INN
VACANCY
I am not concerned with offending God. if there is a final judgment, I will stand in my own defense without pretense or fear.
Until then, let God carry on with his works I shall carry on with mine.
WHUMP WHUMP WHUMP
VLAD! ANSWER THE GODDAMN DOOR!

WE DON'T USUALLY MEET WITH REPORTERS, MISTER MAXWELL.
CALL ME MATT. I UNDERSTAND YOUR RELUCTANCE, BUT I'M NOT HERE FOR A STORY.
I CONTACTED YOU THROUGH YOUR OLD WEBSITE, BUT I'M EMBARRASSED TO ADMIT THAT I DON'T EVEN KNOW YOUR NAMES.
I'M CASSIE. THIS IS VLAD.
TEN BONUS POINTS TO YOU FOR BRINGING COFFEE. I NEEDED THIS.
PLUG THIS INTO YOUR LAPTOP.
I WAS THE FIRST PERSON TO NOTICE THE PATTERN; THE INITIAL INCIDENT WAS THREE WEEKS AGO, AND WRITTEN OFF AS RANDOM WEIRDNESS--
"INCIDENT"?
OH, FUCK BEANS AND BISCUITS.
SOMEONE'S STEALING THE BODIES OF SLASHERS THAT WE'VE KILLED?

WHO'S DOING THIS? AND WHY?!
THE JOBS HAVE BEEN QUICK AND QUIET, AND LIMITED TO YOUR ENEMIES. YOU TWO AREN'T EXACTLY HIGH-PROFILE; IT'S NOT LIKE EVERYONE HAS ACCESS TO THE INFORMATION THEY'D NEED TO PLOT THIS OUT.
SOMETIMES SLASHERS DON'T STAY DEAD. MAYBE THEY ROBBED THEIR OWN GRAVES FROM THE INSIDE...?
THIS IS DEFINITELY AN, UH, "OUTSIDE JOB." ONE CEMETERY HAS SECURITY-CAM FOOTAGE OF SOMEONE COMING ONTO THE GROUNDS AT NIGHT--
PNNNF
SHUKK
SHIT! MATT!
HE'S DEAD.
GEE, YOU THINK?! THIS ISN'T THE TIME TO PLAY "CSI: SHITTY MOTEL," VLAD! WE'VE GOTTA FIND--
--THERE!
HEY! HEY, CHIICKENSHIT WITH THE GUN! WHY DON'TCHA COME BACK AND LET'S DO THIS UP CLOSE, HUH?
DAMN IT, SOMEBODY STOP HER!
BRRRRMNNMNN

ARE THEY FOLLOWING US?
PLEASE. THEY'RE PROBABLY STILL STANDING AROUND YELLING AT--
--Oh.
BATTER UP, BITCH!
BRRRUUUMMM
SHRAAAAAK
Aaahh I CAN'T KEEP IT--
SHREEESH
KROOOOMK
¡¡¡¡XYYAAAAggggh
EEEEEEEETOOMP

WE SHOULD AT LEAST TAKE A PICTURE OF HER FOR THE POLICE OR SOMETHING--
THAT'S THE LAST THING IN THE WORLD YOU SHOULD DO.

THE BRONX.
YOUR HOUSE MAY BE EMPTY, LORD...
...BUT I REMAIN. I STILL LISTEN FOR YOUR VOICE. I WONDER IF YOU KNOW THAT.
I'M CERTAIN HE DOES, EVA.
GOD MAY FALL SILENT FOR A TIME, BUT HE IS EVER-PRESENT. HE REMAINS, JUST AS YOU DO.
AND LIKE HIM, YOU ARE NEVER ALONE.
I KNOW, MICHAEL. YOU'VE STAYED WITH ME LONGER THAN YOU INTENDED...AND PERHAPS LONGER THAN YOU SHOULD.
THE WAR HAS SLOWED, BUT IT'S FAR FROM OVER. I VOWED TO STAND WITH YOU UNTIL THE END, AND I WILL...
...BUT IT IS MORE THAN A PROMISE THAT KEEPS ME WITH YOU.

...THANK YOU.
THE RAIN HAS FINALLY FOUND ITS WAY INSIDE. CAN IT BE MENDED?
I'LL SEE TO IT. HEAVEN KNOWS SOMEONE SHOULD.
HOW COULD THEY DO IT? HOW COULD PEOPLE JUST LEAVE THEIR PLACE OF WORSHIP AND LET IT DECAY LIKE THIS?
THIS IS NOT OUR TIME, AND THEY ARE NOT OUR PEOPLE. THEIR SANCTUARIES ARE DYING BECAUSE THEIR BELIEFS ARE ALREADY DEAD.
I'LL BE IN THE ATTIC. I WANT TO BE CLEAN BEFORE WE MAKE OUR ROUNDS IN THIS FILTHY CITY.
I'D LIKE A MOMENT HERE.
Eh?
WHO'S THERE? STAND FORWARD AND SHOW YOURSELVES.

THIS IS HOLY GROUND, FIENDS...
...I WILL NOT STAND BY AND ALLOW IT TO BE DESECRATED BY THE LIKES OF YOU.
LORD, HEAR MY PRAYER. GRANT ME STRENGTH, AND FORGIVE ME AS I TREAD THE WARRIOR'S PATH IN THIS SACRED HALL.
THY WILL BE DONE.
THE...HERALD...TO FAAA-THERRR.
TO. FA-THER.

YOU ARE UNHOLY ABOMINATIONS--
--AND YOU WILL BE DRIVEN OUT!
EEEYUURYY! BURNNNGH
IIIIIT BUUURRRRNNNNS
GRRM HNNH HNNK
EEEEVAAAAAA

YOU DO NOT BELONG!
I'M HERE! FREE YOURSELF!
HURRNNK!
BACK TO HELL WITH YOU!
HERALD-TO-FATHER!
HUNNH HUUUUUNNNHH HUUUNNHHH
MMMNNNG!
THANK YOU FOR THE RAIN, SWEET LORD. THANK YOU FOR THE RAIN. A BLESSING. A BLESSING.

YOU'RE A FASCINATING LITTLE PATCHWORK MAN, AREN'T YOU?
IT IS AN INDISPUTABLE FACT THAT YOU WERE CREATED BY VICTOR FRANKENSTEIN, AND YET YOU'VE PLEDGED YOUR FAITH TO THE ALL-SEEING FICTION THAT SO MANY BELIEVE TO BE THE CREATOR OF THE ENTIRE HUMAN RACE.
BUT THIS NAME YOU'VE CHOSEN FOR YOURSELF--MICHAEL WAS A CHIEF AMONG THE ANGELS, WASN'T HE? YOU'RE FLIRTING WITH THE SIN OF PRIDE THERE.
ZZZKZZKKZZKKZKZKKZKK
YES. CURIOUS.

WHY DO YOU EXIST? WHAT DRIVES YOU?
TOO STUPID TO SPEAK. TOO STUPID TO RUN AWAY.
HRNK. TO FA..THERRR. HRNK
OKK OKK UNRRK
I STAND CORRECTED ON THE LAST SCORE. DO SAY HELLO TO--
--MICHAEL?!
NNNGH! LET GO OF ME!
OOORR RNNNK
THE RESTRAINTS, EMIL...?
THEY'RE READY, DOCTOR.
SECURE HIM, THEN. LET'S BE ON OUR WAY.

MICHAEL, I'M COMING--
NO! YOU CAN'T...YOU... BRING HIM BACK!
MICHAEL--
CH-HUUKK!
"FATHER." THAT'S A WORD YOU KNOW.
FA. UUOOONK. FAA-K-URRR. FAATH. NNK. FATHER.
YES. TO FATHER. YOU TAKE ME. YO TAKE TO FATHER.

National Constitution Center
Arch St
N 5th St
Race St
N 7th St
Independence Visitor Center
N 4th St
Market St
5th & Market
N 3rd St
Chestnut St
Map data ©2010
DOESN'T FEEL RIGHT. DOESN'T MAKE SENSE.
ACTUALLY, IT MAKES PERFECT SENSE. WHOEVER SENT THOSE FUCKWIT ASSASSINS THIS MORNING OBVIOUSLY HAS CONNECTIONS.
A MAJOR COLLEGE CAMPUS IS A GOOD PLACE TO DICK AROUND WITH DEAD BODIES WITHOUT RAISING AN IMMEDIATE RED FLAG...
...AND I'M GONNA GUESS THIS SECONDARY MAP TO THE "SPECIAL PROJECTS BUILDING" ISN'T GOING TO LEAD US TO A MOTORCYCLE CLASS FOR KIDS WITH PRESCRIPTION HELMETS.
I LIKED HIM. THE GUY WHO GOT KILLED IN OUR MOTEL ROOM. HE WAS COOL.
THINKING ABOUT WHAT HAPPENED TO HIM MAKES ME WANT TO PUKE. THIS KIND OF SHIT JUST PROVES THAT WE WERE RIGHT TO SHUT DOWN HACK/SLASH, INC.
I CAN'T LIVE WITH THE IDEA OF PEOPLE GETTING HURT OR KILLED JUST BECAUSE THEY'RE TRYING TO HELP US.
THIS IS THE PLACE. PUT ON YOUR SNEAKY-PANTS AND LET'S FIND OUT WHAT'S GOING ON HERE.
THEN WE'LL SEE ABOUT SETTLING THE FUCKING SCORE.

--AND THAT'S WHY I'VE ALWAYS INSISTED THAT SCIENCE IS NOT ENOUGH. IF YOU REMOVE THE ART AND THE ROMANCE OF EXPLORATION, YOU ARE LEFT WITH MATH. YOUR END RESULT--
THE "SCIENCE" YOU'RE SEEKING TO PRODUCE--IS ONLY A SUM!
SCIENCE IS NOTHING MORE THAN A BLUNT OBJECT; A GUN, A KNIFE. WHEN YOU STRIKE, YOU NEED A STEADY HAND--
--THE POINT I'M ABOUT TO MAKE IS THE CRUX OF MY ASSERTION, ANA. PAY ATTENTION--
-- BUT TO STRIKE WITH MAXIMUM EFFECT, YOU MUST HAVE PATIENCE!
I'VE BEEN PATIENT. I'VE WAITED LITERALLY HUNDREDS OF YEARS FOR THIS OPPORTUNITY. NO ONE ON EARTH CAN EVEN CONCEIVE OF SUCH A THING...
...WELL, NO ONE EXCEPT THAT GOD-FEARING MONSTROSITY AND HIS RABID VIRGIN LIABILITY. REMIND ME TO HAVE HER KILLED...EH?
GASP!
NO NEED TO WAIT.
WELCOME, EVA. IF YOU'RE EXPECTING ME TO FEIGN SURPRISE BECAUSE YOU TRACKED US HERE, I MAY LEAVE YOU WANTING.
I THINK WE BOTH KNOW THAT YOUR RESOURCEFULNESS HAS NEVER FAILED TO IMPRESS ME.
I KNOW NOTHING OF THE SORT, AND YOUR GAMES ARE TIRING. TAKE ME TO MICHAEL OR DIE AT MY FEET, STRANGER. I HAVE NO PREFERENCE.

YOU CARRY WITH YOU A SPIKE THAT PIERCED THE FLESH OF YOUR SAVIOR WHEN HE HUNG ON THE CROSS...
...BUT YOU'VE FORGOTTEN THE MAN WHO GAVE YOU THAT BLESSED ARTIFACT AND SET YOU ON THE PATH THAT YOU FOLLOW TO THIS DAY.
YOU'RE... NO. YOU CAN'T BE!
I CAN'T BE WHAT?
PRAETORIOUS.
THE VERY SAME.
FIVE HUNDRED YEARS AGO, YOU BROUGHT ME THE MOST POWERFUL OBJECT IN THE HISTORY OF HUMAN EXISTENCE...
...AND EAGERLY TRADED IT AWAY FOR NOTHING MORE THAN A PIECE OF SCRAP METAL MADE LEGENDARY BY THE GREATEST LIE OF ALL TIME.

BLASPHEMER!
STAND--
ASIDEEEII--
AAGGGH--
KRIKIKIK
KRAK
NO HARM SHALL COME TO FATHER.
WHUUUOOOOOUUUGHHH
SKLURRUKK
FLOOR ONE
CASSIE!
I HEARD IT, BUT WHERE--?
DOWNSTAIRS.

I'M SURE YOU ALWAYS INTENDED TO MEET YOUR END WITH MICHAEL AT YOUR SIDE, BUT I'M AFRAID I'M NOT QUITE FINISHED WITH HIM YET.
WH-WHERRE...IS...H-HE? HAVE...I HAVE TO... FUH-FIND HU-U HIMMM...
PHUUHH
IF HEAVEN EXISTS--AND I STILL INSIST IT DOES NOT--I'M AFRAID YOU WON'T EVEN FIND HIM THERE.
ANA...?
KRANNK
YOU TAKE CERTAIN THINGS FOR GRANTED WITH THE EARNEST FAITH OF A CHILD. I ALMOST ADMIRE THAT ABOUT YOU.
FOR EXAMPLE: I'D LIKE TO BELIEVE THAT A JUST AND FAIR GOD WOULD REJECT THE BLOODY CRUSADE YOU'VE CARRIED OUT IN HIS NAME, AND CAST YOU OUT OF HIS KINGDOM AS PUNISHMENT.
BUT I'M A MAN OF SCIENCE. MY OWN BELIEF SYSTEM HAS MORE TANGIBLE REQUIREMENTS. THUS, IF I WANT TO BE CERTAIN THAT YOU'LL SPEND THE REST OF YOUR DAYS BURNING IN HELL...
...THEN I MUST CREATE HELL.

CHOOF
IN THERE. BAD THINGS ARE HAPPENING IN THERE. VERY BAD THINGS...
...LISTEN. DO YOU SMELL SOMETHING?
DOWN CASSIE GETDOWNDOWN DOWN--!
CHOOOOMPH
FUUUUCK MMMMEEEE
BREENT BREENT BREENT BREENT BREENT

koff koff uhuuuk koff
WE HAVE TO Koff GO!
YOU GO. I HAVE TO SEE.
SEE WHAT?! GODDAMMIT, VLAD--
--HOLY SHIT. I GOT HER. RIGHT THERE!
YES. COMING TO US...!
Hnnnn
Hnnuunnngggh
Nnnuuhhnn
KEEP MOVING. WE CAN HELP. GET YOU TO THE HOSPITAL OR SOMETHING. JUST HANG ON. IT'S OKAY. IT'LL BE--
Pray--

ISSUE TWO

CAN YOU HEAR ME?
WHO ARE YOU? WHERE DID YOU COME FROM?
YOU KNOW WHO I AM, MICHAEL.
I DO NOT KNOW YOU. I HAVE NEVER SEEN YOU BEFORE. CAN YOU TELL ME YOUR NAME?
YOUR NAME. PLEASE.
EVA. MY NAME... IS EVA.
HELLO, EVA. I AM VLAD.

VLAD...?! WHERE IS MICHAEL?!
YOUR MASTER DID THIS. PRAETORIOUS DID THIS TO ME! HE TOOK MICHAEL--
I HAVE NO MASTER...
...I DO NOT KNOW MICHAEL OR THIS "PRECARIOUS". MY PARTNER AND I CAME TO THE UNIVERSITY TO FIND A GRAVE ROBBER.
THERE WAS AN EXPLOSION. YOU SURVIVED. BADLY BURNED AND WOUNDED. WE PULLED YOU OUT HERE. TO HELP YOU--
GOD FORGIVE ME! MY CLOTHING... I AM NOT TO BE SEEN LIKE THIS!
I...I PUT A BLANKET ON YOU.
HAVE TO GO-- Uuaauuughh!
YOU CAN NOT GO YET. I THINK YOU ARE HEALING YOURSELF, BUT IT IS GOING TOO SLOWLY. WE WILL TAKE CARE OF YOU UNTIL YOU ARE WELL.
AND I WILL COVER YOU, I PROMISE...
NYU CAMPUS, NEW YORK CITY

HEY! QUIT PLAYING TAILGATE DOCTOR AND LET'S ROLL! CHOP CHOP!
SHE WOKE UP, CASSIE. I WAS TRYING TO CALM HER DOWN.
GOOD JOB. I MANAGED TO GET SOME PRETTY CHOICE LEADS, BUT THE COPS AND FIRE DEPARTMENT SHOWED UP...
...SO UNLESS YOU CAN CALM DOWN A FUCKING S.W.A.T. TEAM, WE NEED TO HIT THE ROAD RIGHT NOW.
WEST
INTERSTATE
80
OKAY, WE KNOW SOMEONE IN THAT SCIENCE BUILDING WAS DIGGING UP SOME OF OUR DEAD SLASHERS AND KILLING PEOPLE FOR FINDING OUT ABOUT IT.
WE'RE ON THE SCENE FOR TEN MINUTES WHEN ONE OF THE LABS JUST FUCKING EXPLODES. THAT'S NO COINCIDENCE.
THE LAB BELONGED TO A PROFESSOR PIOTR RUSEA. HE HAD A SEPARATE OFFICE UPSTAIRS, SO I WENT DIGGING IN HIS PRIVATE FILES.
THIS IS OUR GUY. HE'S BEEN SHIPPING VERY LARGE, EXPENSIVE ITEMS TO AN ADDRESS IN DETROIT FOR THE LAST YEAR OR SO.
EVERY ITEM HAS ITS OWN SET OF SPECIAL INSTRUCTIONS, TOO. "LIVE SPECIMEN"... "TEMPERATURE CONTROL"... "VACUUM SEALED CONTAINER."
I MEAN SERIOUSLY.

I AM WORRIED ABOUT THE GIRL. ABOUT EVA.
HER WOUNDS WERE TERRIBLE, BUT HER BODY SEEMS TO BE FIXING ITSELF. THAT IS GOOD, BUT...
YEAH, THAT IS GOOD.
...SHE WAS ANGRY AND CONFUSED. WHAT HAPPENS WHEN SHE HAS HEALED? I DID NOT DO A GOOD JOB OF CALMING HER DOWN.
YEAH, SHE'S GONNA BE SERIOUSLY PISSED OFF WHEN SHE WAKES UP IN THE BACK OF A HEARSE, ROLLING AROUND NAKED WITH ALL OUR CLOTHES AND SUPPLIES.
AND WEAPONS.
AND WEAPONS.
PULL OVER, VLAD.
VLAAAAAAD!

WHUMP
I'VE GOT HER! PULL OVER!
MMMGH!
BRAKES.
EVA, CALM DOWN. WE CAN HELP YOU!
LIAR! YOU'RE A SERVANT OF PRAETORIOUS! NOW TELL ME WHERE HE'S KEEPING MICHAEL!
I'M GONNA SAY THIS ONE TIME, LADY:
WE. DO. NOT. KNOW. WHAT. YOU'RE. TALKING. ABOUT.
...BUT I THINK WE MAY BE LOOKING FOR THE SAME ASSHOLE, IN A MANNER OF SPEAKING. CAN WE DISCUSS THIS WITH CLOTHES ON AND NO KNIVES?
SO BE IT.

DETROIT, MICHIGAN
12:15 PM
NO, NO. HE IS A MARVELOUS CREATION, BUT I CANNOT CLAIM HIM.
FATHER? MADE THIS?
KEEP THAT CARRIER STEADY ONCE THE ELEVATOR STARTS MOVING. IT TENDS TO JOLT A LITTLE BIT.
DOCTOR PRAETORIOUS DIDN'T GO TO THE TROUBLE OF CAPTURING THAT MONSTER JUST TO HAVE HIM DAMAGED ON ARRIVAL.
TRUE ENOUGH, EMIL. ANA AND I WILL SEE YOU AT THE MAIN SITE SOON, I TRUST?
YES, DOCTOR. SHALL I STERILIZE THIS LOCATION?
NOT JUST YET. LET'S KEEP OUR OPTIONS OPEN.

3:15 P.M.
IF OUR RAT WAS EVER HERE, HE'S SCURRIED OFF BY NOW.
WE SHOULD DEFINITELY CHECK THE PLACE OUT FROM TOP TO BOTTOM, BUT I'M NOT OPTIMISTIC.
IF YOU TWO HAVE ANY BRIGHT IDEAS, NOW WOULD BE THE TIME TO SOUND OFF.
I HAVE A KIND OF... SPECIAL SIGHT.
I CAN SENSE THE DARKNESS THAT HIDES WITHIN A SOUL. SOMETIMES WHEN A BEING BEARS THE MARK OF PURE EVIL, THEY EMIT A UNIQUELY FOUL SPIRITUAL SIGNATURE.
PRAETORIOUS WAS HERE. PERHAPS I SHOULD BE THANKFUL I DIDN'T HAVE TO FACE HIM WEARING THESE...HARLOT SCARVES!
YOU WANTED CLOTHES, I GAVE YOU CLOTHES. I'M SORRY YOU THINK I DRESS LIKE A SLUT, EVA, BUT THIS IS THE 21ST CENTURY! WOMEN DON'T RUN AROUND WITH A GOD-LOCK ON THEIR CROTCHES!
A WHORE'S MOUTH TO MATCH A WHORE'S HEART--
--YOU'RE ABOUT TO TAKE A WHORE'S BOOT TO THE HEAD, SISTER MARY STICK-IN-YOUR-ASS.
HRRN. STOP. NOW.

CHECK IT OUT, YO! I THINK I SEE A COUPLE OF TRICKS LOOKIN' FOR A TREAT.
HEY, WHY DON'T YOU BABIES LOSE THAT FREAKY MISTER POTATO HEAD AND LET US SHOW YOU HOW THE LONE WOLVES DO IT, HUH?
MR. POTATO WILL RIP YOUR ARMS OFF AND SEND YOU HOME TO MOTHER, YES?
HANG ON. YOU'RE THE LONE WOLVES? YOU DO KNOW THAT "LONE" MEANS "NOT IN A GROUP," RIGHT? ARE YOU ONE OF THOSE SHORT BUS GANGS?
OH, SHIT. YOU DIDN'T JUST GO THERE. TWO THINGS, CHICA:
YOU DON'T FRONT ON OUR NAME, AND YOU DON'T MAKE RUDE JOKES ABOUT PEOPLE WITH SPECIAL NEEDS. FOR REAL.
THAT'S KIND OF A STRANGE POINT TO GET ALL HUFFY ABOUT, BUT...OH. I SEE.
WHAT'S UP WITH THE CAMERA, STEVEN SPECIAL-BERG?
I LIKE TO MAKE WEREWOLF MOVIES.
AW, WENDELL. WE TOLD YOU TO KEEP THAT SHIT QUIET!

GO PLAY IN TRAFFIC, PUPPY CHOW. WE'VE GOT GROWN-UP STUFF TO DO.
YOUR FRIEND WAS RIGHT. YOU GOT A WHORE'S MOUTH. TALKIN' THAT KINDA MESS GONNA GET YOU HURT.
YO, SHOW THESE BITCHES HOW WE TREAT...UH... BITCHES.
WE ARE STILL GOING TO INVESTIGATE, YES? I SHOULD GET THE TOOLBOX?
JEEZ, I ALMOST FORGOT.
HEY! TURN AROUND AND SEE WHAT YOU'VE DONE!
I HAVE NO MORE PATIENCE FOR THIS--
UUUAAAAOOOOOO
QUIET ON THE SET!
WENDELL, PLEASE. BE COOL, MAN.
SORRY, MIGUEL.

AAANNNND... ACTION!
GGRRRAAAAAAGGGH
EVA! CASSIE!
WELL MET.
YOU'VE DONE THIS BEFORE, RIGHT?
I WAS KILLING WEREWOLVES BEFORE YOU WERE BORN.
FIVE CENTURIES BEFORE YOU WERE BORN, IN FACT. SO, YES...I'VE "GOT THIS."
RROAAAUGGH
SHRUUK

WHUUH--
EEEYYYAAAAH
GETOFFGET OFFLETGO
CASSANDRA! I AM COMING!
GRR
NNNGGGH
FILTHY HELLHOUND!
SHREEEEENK
MMEEUUMF
SHUNK
SHUNK
JESUS GET IT OFF ME IT HURTS IT HUUURRTS
Hunnh Hunnnh Hunnh
THEIR LEADER... WHERE IS HE?
AAIIIOOOOOOAAAAAH

AIIOONH! AOOORNH!
Y'KNOW, I KINDA REGRET MAKING FUN OF THEIR GANG NAME NOW.
LET THEM COME. TWO OR TWO HUNDRED, IT DOESN'T MATTER.
I AM SORRY I DID NOT PROTECT YOU.
BOTH OF YOU.
KILL THE FREAK. MAKE THE WOMEN BLEED AND WEEP, BUT LEAVE THEM ALIVE.
I WANT TO PLAY WITH THEM BEFORE THEY DIE.

DO YOU HEAR THAT?
YEAH. SOUNDS LIKE THUNDER.
AW, HELL NO.
I KNEW THIS WAS GONNA HAPPEN. I KNEW IT--
WENDELL, GET DOWUUAAGH--
BRAAAAAP
BRAPAP
BRAPAP
BRAAAAAP
BRAPAP
BRAPAP
BRAPAP
THAT IS NOT THUNDER.
BRAPAP
BRAPAP
AAAWWOOOOOOOOOOO
BRAAAAAP

BRAAAAAP
BRAAAAAP
RUN, YOU LITTLE BASTARDS! RUN AND HIDE!
BRAPAP
BRAPAP
BRAPAP
BRAPAP
BRAPAP
BRAAAAAP
BRAPAP
BRRUUUUMMMMMM

I DON'T FEEL SO Goooooood--
YOU HAVE LOST MUCH BLOOD. REST NOW.
EVA? WHAT ARE YOU DOING?
STUPID CAMERA. STUPID GHOSTS. HAVE TO FINISH THE MOVIE. HAVE TO FINISH IT.
GONNA NEED A SCREWDRIVER--
AIIEEEE!
WOLF OR NOT, YOU RUN WITH THEM BY CHOICE. THEIR SINS ARE YOURS, AND THEIR PUNISHMENT AS WELL.
NO!
SPRANG

YOU CANNOT KILL THIS BOY! HE DOES NOT UNDERSTAND. HE CAN NOT UNDERSTAND!
Eeiijuuuh. Eeuh. Eeuh.
I DIDN'T REALIZE. MERCIFUL GOD, YOU...THANK YOU FOR STEPPING IN.
THANK YOU FOR NOT STABBING ME.
THEY'RE COMING BACK.
GHOSTS. THEY'RE THE GHOSTS.
THESE ARE NOT GHOSTS. THEY ARE VERY REAL.
NAAH, THE KID'S GOT IT RIGHT. WE ARE THE GHOSTS. I MEAN, WE'RE TOTALLY REAL AND NOT DEAD OR ANYTHING LIKE THAT, BUT...
...SORRY, I'M BABBLING. POST-WEREWOLF-CHASE ADRENALINE RUSH. MY NAME'S EUGENE. YOU GUYS HAVE A FEW MINUTES TO TALK?

"SORRY, BUT I STILL DON'T UNDERSTAND THIS WHOLE 'GHOST' THING."
GHOSTS OF OLD DETROIT. WE'RE KIND OF A PRIVATE SECURITY COMPANY.
ACTUALLY, "COMPANY" IMPLIES THAT WE GET PAID, OR HAVE ACTUAL RESOURCES. PRIVATE ARMY, MAYBE? CAN FIVE PEOPLE BE AN ARMY?
GOOD WORK, NORD. NOW EVEN I'M CONFUSED.
I'M CALLED SHEPHERD. THIS IS MY BROTHER J.R., AND THAT'S COEY. YOU MET EUGENE ALREADY.
YOU'RE IN A PARTICULARLY HORRIBLE AREA OF DETROIT THAT THE LOCALS CALL SHADOWTOWN. I GUESS YOU COULD CONSIDER US THE VOLUNTEER POLICE DEPARTMENT.
HONESTLY, THE REGULAR COPS AREN'T WILLING OR ABLE TO DEAL WITH THE WEIRD SHIT WE'VE GOT KICKIN' AROUND DOWN HERE.
THE REASONS THAT BROUGHT US HERE MIGHT ACTUALLY TOP THE WEIRD SHIT LIST--
--AND YES, I REALIZE I'M TALKING TO PEOPLE WHO FIGHT WEREWOLF STREET GANGS--
--SO IF YOU KNOW WHERE THE MAD SCIENTISTS HANG OUT, WE'D LOVE TO HEAR ABOUT IT.
THIS MAD SCIENTIST OF YOURS...DOES HE HAPPEN TO MAKE PEOPLE OUT OF CLAY?
YES! YES!

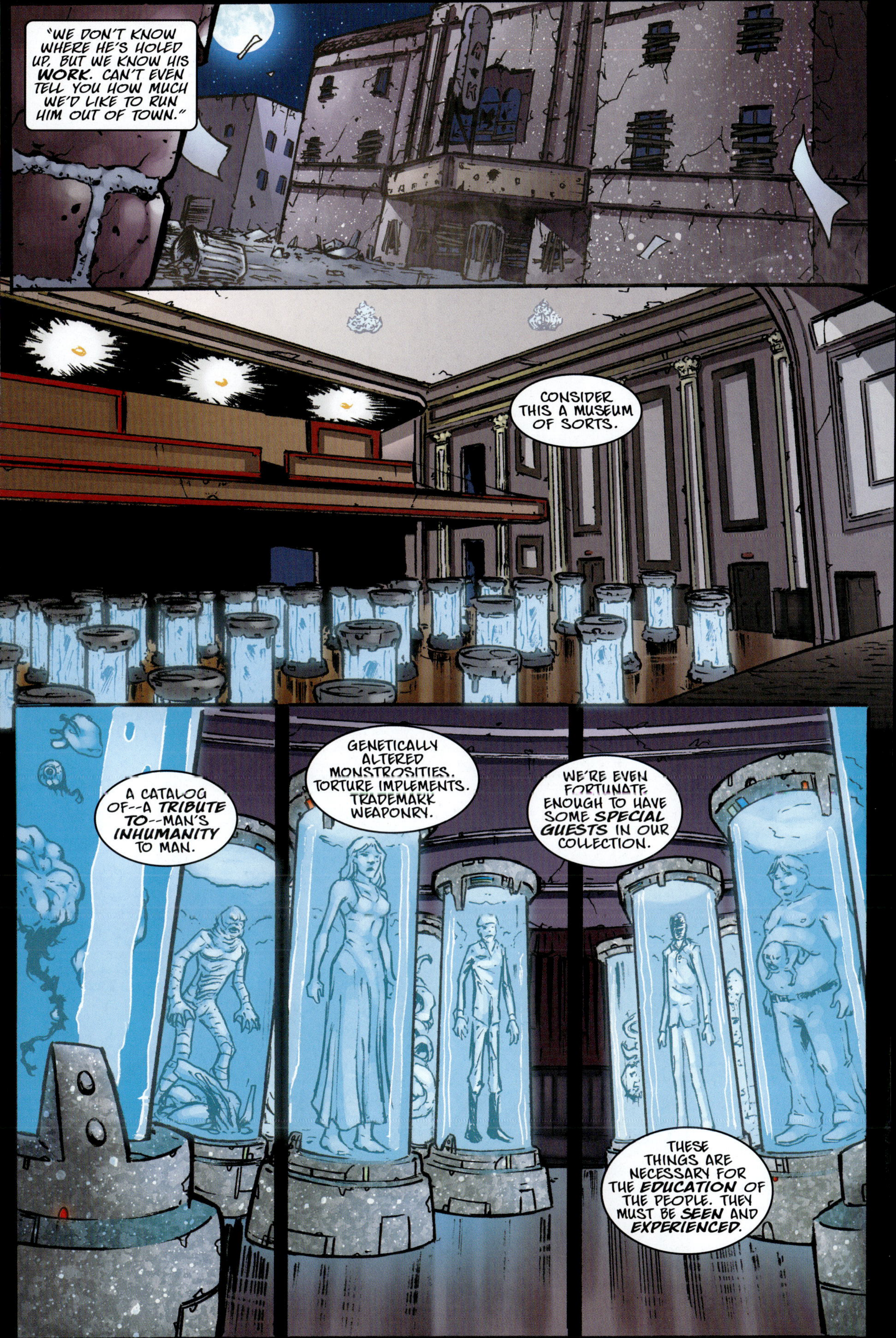
"WE DON'T KNOW WHERE HE'S HOLED UP, BUT WE KNOW HIS **WORK**. CAN'T EVEN TELL YOU HOW MUCH WE'D LIKE TO RUN HIM OUT OF TOWN."
CONSIDER THIS A MUSEUM OF SORTS.
A CATALOG OF--A ***TRIBUTE TO***--MAN'S ***INHUMANITY*** TO MAN.
GENETICALLY ALTERED MONSTROSITIES. TORTURE IMPLEMENTS. TRADEMARK WEAPONRY.
WE'RE EVEN FORTUNATE ENOUGH TO HAVE SOME ***SPECIAL GUESTS*** IN OUR COLLECTION.
THESE THINGS ARE NECESSARY FOR THE ***EDUCATION*** OF THE PEOPLE. THEY MUST BE ***SEEN*** AND ***EXPERIENCED***.

YOU SEE ANYTHING DOWN THERE?
COEY? EUGENE? DO YOU COPY?
SHEPHERD, YOU ARE NEVER GOING TO BELIEVE THIS ONE. I THINK YOU ALL NEED TO HEAD DOWN HERE AND CHECK IT OUT FOR YOURSELVES.
YOU HEARD THE LADY. IT'S GO-TIME.
GO-TIME? WHAT HAPPENS NOW?
NOW YOU HAVE TO GO HOME, WENDELL. YOU'VE BEEN A BIG HELP TODAY, BUT I WANT YOU TO PROMISE ME YOU'LL GO HOME AND STAY THERE UNTIL YOU HEAR FROM US, OKAY?
YEAH. OKAY. I GUESS.
ONE MORE THING: LADIES, I JUST CAN'T GO MARCHING INTO A HOT-ZONE WITH YOU TWO LOOKING LIKE THE PUSSYCAT DOLLS...NO OFFENSE.
I'M GONNA NEED YOU TO PUT ON SOME PROPER GEAR.

FOR ALL HIS FAULTS, VICTOR FRANKENSTEIN WAS A GENIUS. YOUR CREATOR DESERVES ONLY THE HIGHEST OF PRAISE.
YOU HAVE A STRANGE WAY OF SHOWING RESPECT FOR HIS WORK. WHAT DO YOU PLAN TO DO WITH ME?
I'M GOING TO HELP YOU REACH YOUR FULL POTENTIAL, MICHAEL. JUST AS VICTOR INTENDED.
YOU CARRY A SECRET WITHIN YOUR CONSTRUCTION.
IT IS A HIDDEN FUNCTION THAT WILL ALLOW ME TO CREATE NEW LIFE OUT OF THE DEAD MATERIAL OF MANKIND'S FAILURE.
I'M BEING RUDE. I HAVEN'T EVEN INTRODUCED YOU TO MY COLLABORATOR IN THIS GRAND UNDERTAKING. ANA, IF YOU WOULD...?

THIS MAY BE CONFUSING AT FIRST, BUT I PROMISE I'LL EXPLAIN EVERYTHING. MICHAEL, PLEASE SAY HELLO TO YOUR OTHER CREATOR...
...MARY SHELLEY LOVECRAFT.

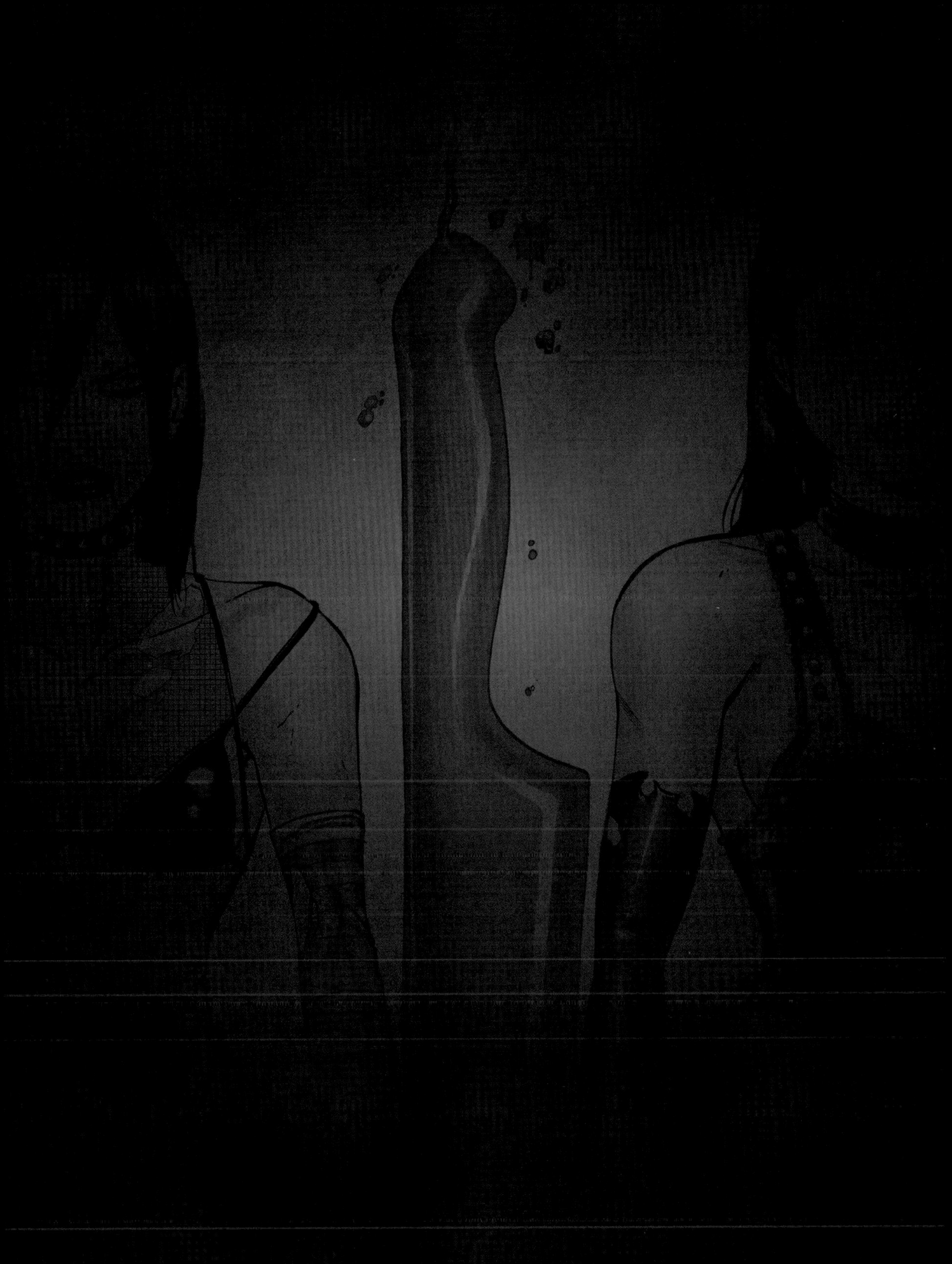

ISSUE THREE

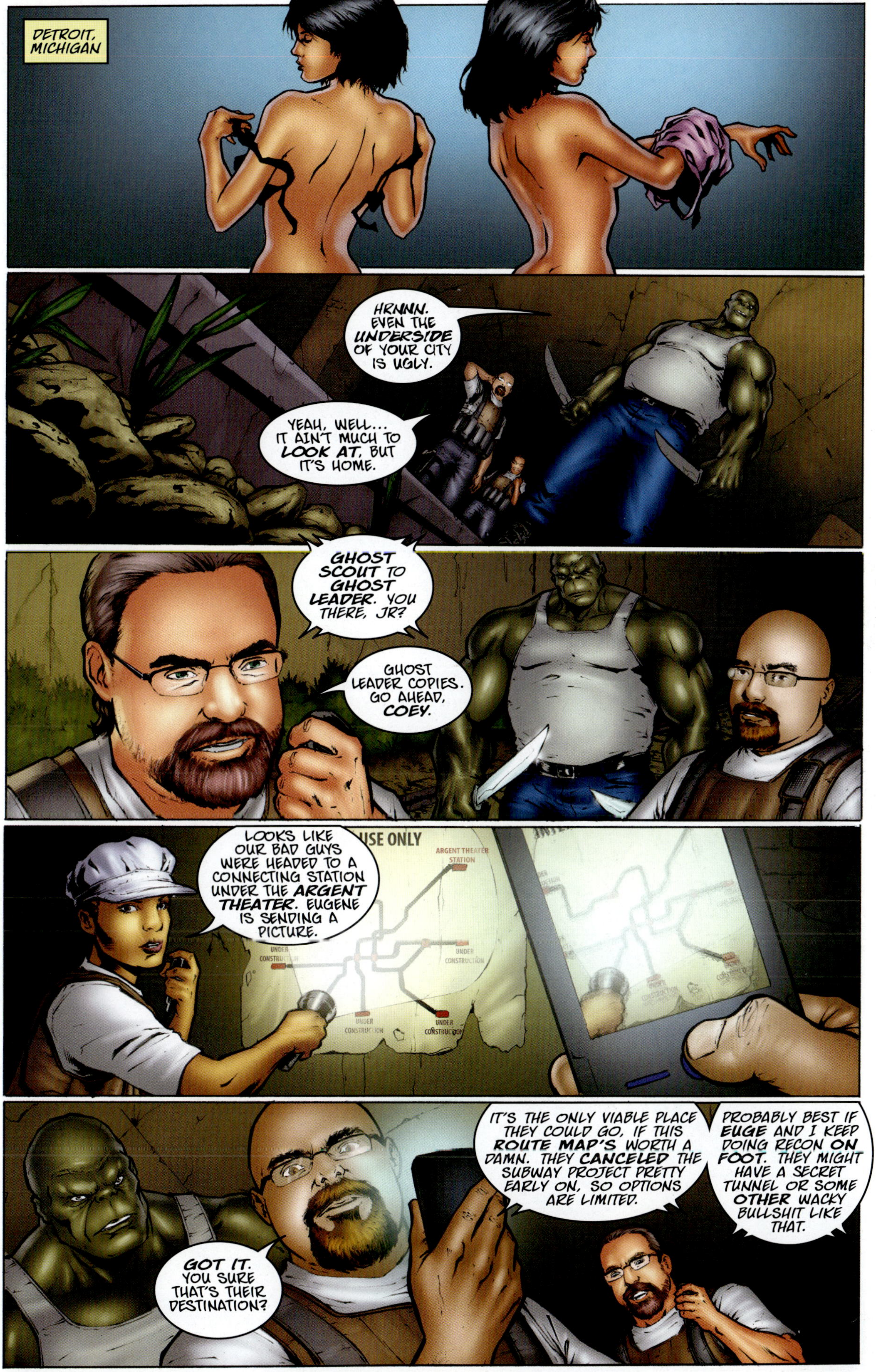
DETROIT, MICHIGAN
HRNNN. EVEN THE UNDERSIDE OF YOUR CITY IS UGLY.
YEAH, WELL... IT AIN'T MUCH TO LOOK AT, BUT IT'S HOME.
GHOST SCOUT TO GHOST LEADER. YOU THERE, JR?
GHOST LEADER COPIES. GO AHEAD, COEY.
LOOKS LIKE OUR BAD GUYS WERE HEADED TO A CONNECTING STATION UNDER THE ARGENT THEATER. EUGENE IS SENDING A PICTURE.
USE ONLY
ARGENT THEATER STATION
UNDER CONSTRUCTION
UNDER CONSTRUCTION
UNDER CONSTRUCTION
UNDER CONSTRUCTION
IT'S THE ONLY VIABLE PLACE THEY COULD GO, IF THIS ROUTE MAP'S WORTH A DAMN. THEY CANCELED THE SUBWAY PROJECT PRETTY EARLY ON, SO OPTIONS ARE LIMITED.
PROBABLY BEST IF EUGE AND I KEEP DOING RECON ON FOOT. THEY MIGHT HAVE A SECRET TUNNEL OR SOME OTHER WACKY BULLSHIT LIKE THAT.
GOT IT. YOU SURE THAT'S THEIR DESTINATION?

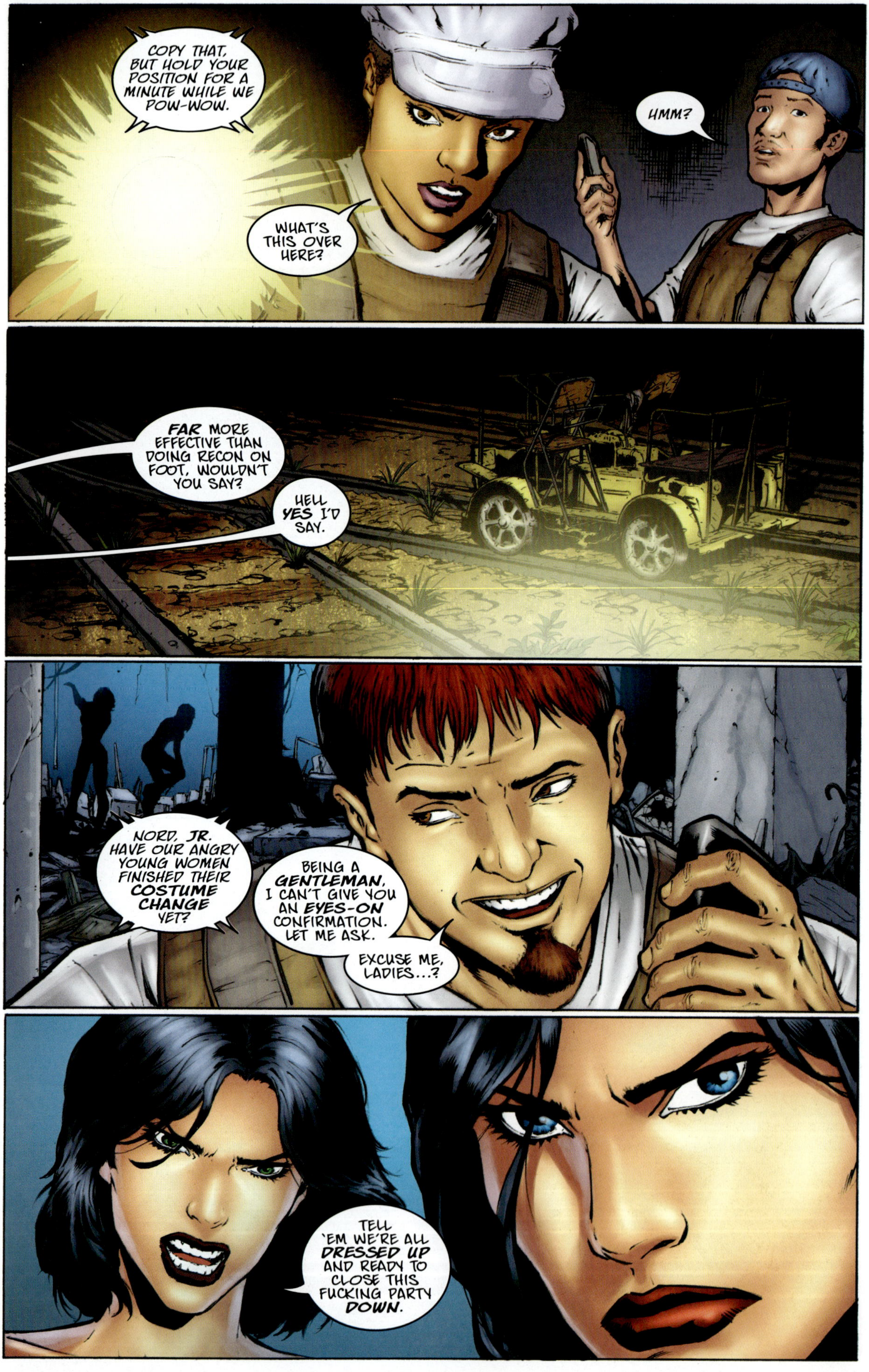
COPY THAT, BUT HOLD YOUR POSITION FOR A MINUTE WHILE WE POW-WOW.
UMM?
WHAT'S THIS OVER HERE?
FAR MORE EFFECTIVE THAN DOING RECON ON FOOT, WOULDN'T YOU SAY?
HELL YES I'D SAY.
NORD, JR. HAVE OUR ANGRY YOUNG WOMEN FINISHED THEIR COSTUME CHANGE YET?
BEING A GENTLEMAN, I CAN'T GIVE YOU AN EYES-ON CONFIRMATION. LET ME ASK.
EXCUSE ME, LADIES...?
TELL 'EM WE'RE ALL DRESSED UP AND READY TO CLOSE THIS FUCKING PARTY DOWN.

PERMISSION TO SPEAK FREELY, GHOST LEADER?
WHAT? GO AHEAD, NORD.
CASSIE AND EVA ARE READY TO ROLL...
...AND THEY ARE LOOKING PRETTY GODDAMN STELLAR FROM WHERE I'M STANDING.
...UH, COPY THAT.

AW, SHIT. YOU SEE THAT?
NAH, I DON'T KNOW 'EM. WHO IT IS?
THE GHOSTS OF OLD MOTHERFUCKIN' DETROIT, MAN. IF THEY DOWN HERE...
...THEN SHIT'S ABOUT TO GET REAL. I MEAN REAL REAL.

UH-OH.
WHAT?

THAT.
OH. YEAH. TIME TO GO.

THE ARGENT THEATER
MY SCIENTIFIC CURIOSITY--MY HUNGER FOR KNOWLEDGE--HAS ALWAYS BEEN INSATIABLE, BUT THERE WERE SOME CONCEPTS THAT EVEN I NEVER THOUGHT TO QUESTION.
THE NATURE OF REALITY WAS SOMETHING I ACCEPTED AT FACE VALUE. MORE EXISTENTIAL SCIENTISTS WERE PROBING THE MYSTERY, BUT I COULDN'T BE BOTHERED...
...UNTIL I MET MARY SHELLEY LOVECRAFT. HER BEAUTIFUL PSYCHE REACHED ACROSS MULTIPLE DIMENSIONS AND HELD ME IN ITS THRALL. SHE OPENED MY MIND WITH HER OWN.
ENOUGH STORYTELLING, PRAETORIOUS! MAKE YOUR INTENTIONS KNOWN--
RRNNNGH!
A RIPPLE IN THE FABRIC. A FAMILIAR HAND TUGGING AT THE CURTAIN.

CASSANDRA, THE DESPISED. SHE IS COMING. SHE IS NOT ALONE. HER PROTECTOR WALKS WITH HER, SIDE BY SIDE WITH THE DAUGHTER OF THE DRAGON AND A SPIRIT BROTHERHOOD.
THEY SEEK A SHAPING OF REALITY THROUGH VIOLENT ACTIONS.
CASSANDRA MUST NOT BE PERMITTED TO HARM ME AGAIN, PRAETORIOUS. YOU GAVE YOUR WORD.
I DID INDEED, BUT YOU HAD A SPECIFIC FATE IN MIND FOR HACK AND HER MONSTROUS MAJORDOMO. HOW WOULD YOU HAVE ME DEAL WITH THIS PROBLEM?
THIN THE RANKS AROUND THEM, DOCTOR. MAKE THEIR ALLIES YOUR VICTIMS...
...BUT CASSIE AND VLAD MUST BE LEFT AT DEATH'S DOOR AND TAKEN NO FURTHER. THEY ARE MINE TO FINISH.
SO BE IT. YOU HEARD HER WISH, EMIL. NOW...
...UNLEASH THE MENAGERIE!

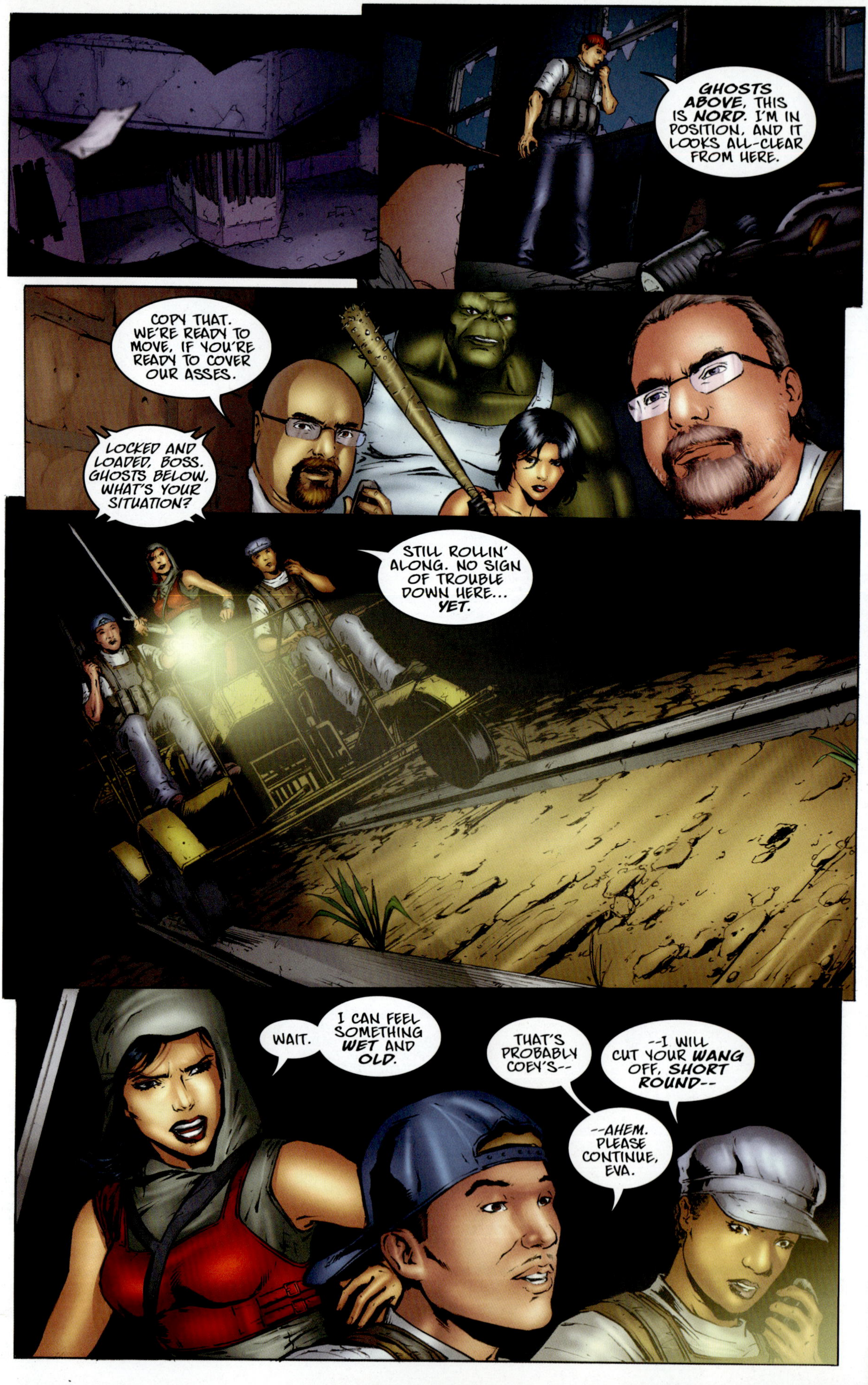
GHOSTS ABOVE, THIS IS NORD. I'M IN POSITION, AND IT LOOKS ALL-CLEAR FROM HERE.
COPY THAT. WE'RE READY TO MOVE, IF YOU'RE READY TO COVER OUR ASSES.
LOCKED AND LOADED, BOSS. GHOSTS BELOW, WHAT'S YOUR SITUATION?
STILL ROLLIN' ALONG. NO SIGN OF TROUBLE DOWN HERE... YET.
WAIT.
I CAN FEEL SOMETHING WET AND OLD.
THAT'S PROBABLY COEY'S--
--I WILL CUT YOUR WANG OFF, SHORT ROUND--
--AHEM. PLEASE CONTINUE, EVA.

THERE! THE LIGHT...!
WET, HUH? I DO HEAR WATER--
--AW, MAN! YOU SMELL THAT? LIKE THE SHIT THAT SHIT WOULD SHIT!
YOUSEETHAT?!
SPANG
BRAK AKA KAK
SHEPHERD! NORD! EVERYBODY! WE'VE GOT TROUBLE NOW!

JESUS, WHAT'S HAPPENING DOWN THERE?!
MONSTERS. HRRRN. **MONSTERS** ARE HAPPENING.
WE COULDN'T **GET** TO THEM IN TIME TO HELP IF WE **WANTED** TO. WE HAVE TO MOVE ON THE THEATER...
...NOW!
COME ONE, COME ALL! BASK IN THE GLORIOUS **SPECTACLE!**
THE ACCOUNT OF THIS DAY WILL BE **TRANSCRIBED** IN THE INK OF YOUR BLOO--
UUURRRBLGH
KRAK
SPUK
NICE SHOT, NORD. QUALITY WORK.
THANKS. I COULD'VE LET YOU ALL HANG FOR ANOTHER HALF-A-MINUTE, BUT I THINK NICK-OF-TIME RESCUES ARE A HUGE LOAD OF HORSESHIT, Y'KNOW?

LET'S TRY THIS AGAIN. KEEP YOUR EYES PEELED FOR MORE... UH...NAKED ASSHOLES.
FOUND ONE!
URK. Shrkurrrhuuk. MMNNNGHAAH.
YOU...YOU INTERRUPTED ME. I SHOULD--I SHOULD START AG-AGAIN. BUT I C-CAN'T--LET ME JUST--JUST SA-SA-SAY THISSSS.
IT'S SHOWTIME!
shhhrrrrr
kkikikik
ALL THIS CRAZY SHIT GOING ON, AND I STILL CAN'T STOP LOOKING AT HIS DICK.
I KNOW. GOD HELP ME, I KNOW.
HUUEEHEEHEHEE
UURRK
UUHHEEHEEEEE
YAAAAAAAAAH
SKRRIIIIPPPP
SSPLIIIKKK
UUUUUUUUK

AAAUGH! RELEASE! YOU ARE FREE!
SHKREEEEE

From the journals of Victor Frankenstein:
We are, all of us, monsters in one fashion or another. We deceive, we betray, we harm, we kill.
We wage war against our neighbors for selfish reasons that even we cannot recall, for they are ancient prejudices from lost generations.
We justify the most brutal of actions by ascribing to them the necessity of survival.
Life, when pressed or threatened, inevitably discovers a new path to perpetuity. Am I a monster, then, for seeking a new path to creation?
Or am I guided now as an instrument, unwittingly serving life's quest to endure?
Let the others make war, and leave death in their wake. My mission is the antithesis of theirs, and I am pleased by it.

REGROUP BACK AT THE RENDEZVOUS POINT--
Grrgyaaayyyyaaah
NO!
JR, TRY TO HOLD STILL! I'VE ALMOST GOT THE LITTLE FUCKER--
Nnn fffffucking teethjesus ithurts
OFF! GET OFF HIM! LET GO!
EEEA YYYAAAAH
GODDAMN IT, TOM. FOCUS. FOCUS. YOU CAN DO THIS...
HURRRR NNNNNNGG GGGU
CHU-SHLUUK
JOEY! JESUS CHRIST, JOEY, I'M COMING--

BAD ENOUGH WE JUST WRESTLED ALLIGATOR DUDES THAT RAN UP ON US FROM A SEWER TUNNEL...
...BUT THEY SCREWED US OUT OF OUR GETAWAY CAR. I HOPE WE DON'T NEED TO HAUL ASS OUT OF HERE AT A HIGH RATE OF SPEED, GIRLS.
IF YOU CAN RUN YOUR FEET LIKE YOU RUN YOUR MOUTH, YOU'LL BE OUTTA HERE LIKE FLOJO.
NRRK RRRMM
I'VE FOUGHT THEIR KIND BEFORE. THEY FALL, BUT NOT WITHOUT CONSIDERABLE EFFORT.
WE CANNOT AFFORD ANY MORE DELAYS. MICHAEL NEEDS ME.
GO FIND YOUR FRIEND. WE'LL HANDLE THIS.
BRAKAKA KAK
VICTOR FRANKENSTEIN WAS NO FOOL, MICHAEL. HE KNEW EXACTLY WHAT HE WAS DOING WHEN HE CHOSE TO CONCEAL HIS GREATEST SECRET WITHIN HIS GREATEST CREATION.
A FOOL WOULD HAVE BURIED IT DEEP, BUT VICTOR KNEW THAT SOMEONE MIGHT COME LOOKING ONE DAY. CUT TOO ZEALOUSLY, AND YOU DAMAGE THE PRIZE...
...BECAUSE IT'S JUST BENEATH THE SURFACE.
THE RETRACTOR, ANA.

THERE IT IS. WITH MY OWN EYES, I SEE IT...
...AND WITH MY OWN TWO HANDS, I TAKE POSSESSION OF IT. OH, I HAVE WAITED SO MANY LIFETIMES FOR THIS MOMENT.
tnk tnk
THE DARK ONE. THE DARK DAUGHTER. SHE IS DRAWING EVER CLOSER, DOCTOR... SHE IS...
SHE IS HERE...
...AND SHE HAS COME TO END YOU!

ANA!
THY WILL BE DONE, DOCTOR.
SKRIISHAK
WHAT MANNER OF HELLBRIDE ARE YOU?!
HELL IS A SUPERSTITIOUS CONSEQUENCE FROM A LONG-DEAD AGE; FICTION TO KEEP THE FLOCK FROM JUMPING THE FENCE.
NNNNGSH!!
BRAKAKAKAK
WHAT IS THIS?
I DON'T KNOW WHAT YOU ARE, BUT YOU NEED TO DROP THAT GIRL AND BACK UP. YOU WANNA DO THAT RIGHT THE HELL NOW, TOO.
LEAVE THEM, MARY!
BAH!

THEY'VE ALREADY TAKEN ANA FROM US. WE CAN'T LET THEM IMPEDE OUR PLANS NOW!
COME WITH ME. I'LL SHOW YOU.
I HAVE TO GO TO HIM. I HAVE TO KNOW--
WHAT ABOUT THE FREAKS WHO WERE HOLDING HIM CAPTIVE?
WE JUST LETTING THEM SKATE OUT OF HERE?!
YO, GHOSTS! WHAT'S YOUR TWENTY? WE'VE GOT TWO BIG BADS TRYING TO SNEAK OUT THE BACK.
SPAK
LET 'EM GO. WE HAVE BIGGER PROBLEMS.
EVA.
WHAT DID THEY DO TO YOU? WHAT DID THAT DEVIL SUBJECT YOU TO, MICHAEL?!
SHEPHERD? WHERE IS EVERYBODY...?
OH, GOD. IT'S BAD, ISN'T IT?

TRINITY MEDICAL CL
CAREFUL. MOVE HIM SLOWLY.
I'M SURE WE CAN FIGURE OUT A WAY TO HELP HIM, EVA.
HE WILL ENDURE, IF GOD WILLS IT. WE MUST BELIEVE.
UH, SURE. OKAY.
HEADS UP, PEOPLE. WE'VE GOT COMPANY.
Police
Detroit Police
WHAT WAS THAT, EXACTLY?
THE COPS JUST DRIVE BY AND MAKE SURE YOU'VE GOT THINGS HANDLED WITHOUT THEM?
WE CAME TO AN UNDERSTANDING WITH THE DETROIT POLICE DEPARTMENT A LONG TIME AGO. THEY HANDLE THE NORMAL NASTINESS HERE IN SHADOWTOWN...
...AND WE TAKE CARE OF THE TRULY HORRIBLE SHIT THAT THEY'RE NOT CAPABLE OF WRAPPING THEIR HEADS AROUND.
LISTEN TO YOURSELF, WOMAN! HOW CAN YOUR CONSCIENCE ALLOW SUCH MADNESS TO SPILL FROM YOUR LIPS?!

YOU FIGHT TO SAFEGUARD A CITY OF WASTE AND SINFUL DESPAIR, SURROUNDED BY GODLESS HEATHENS AND MORALLY BEREFT LAYABOUTS!
YOUR PRIESTS ARE CHARLATANS AND YOUR CONSTABLES ARE COWARDS--
SHPOK
MY MOTHER WAS A MINISTER AND MY FATHER WAS A COP. A PRIEST AND A CONSTABLE, AS YOU SAY. THEY BOTH DIED DOING EVERYTHING THEY COULD TO FIX THIS CITY.
I APPRECIATE YOUR FAITH AND I RESPECT YOUR FIRE...
...BUT THIS IS OUR WORLD, AND WE'RE DOING EVERYTHING WE CAN TO KEEP IT FROM BURNING DOWN TO THE GROUND.
I HOPE WE CAN ALL BE BETTER PEOPLE SOMEDAY. I PRAY EVERY NIGHT THAT WE CAN TURN THIS AROUND. RIGHT NOW, WE'RE JUST HOLDING THE LINE.
YOU RISKED EVERYTHING TO RESCUE YOUR FRIEND. WE BOTH KNOW THAT MOST PEOPLE LOOK AT HIM AND SEE A MONSTER WHO'S NOT WORTH SAVING, BUT YOU KNOW DIFFERENT, DON'T YOU?
YES.
NOW YOU KNOW HOW WE FEEL ABOUT DETROIT.

ARE YOU IN PAIN?
NOT MUCH.
YOUR FRIEND THOMAS IS A VERY CAPABLE CAREGIVER.
THANKS, MICHAEL. I'M TRYING.
THERE'S SOMETHING YOU NEED TO KNOW, EVA. VICTOR--MY FATHER--ENTRUSTED ME WITH A SECRET THAT I NEVER THOUGHT ANYONE WOULD DISCOVER.
FATHER PLACED SOMETHING WITHIN MY WORKINGS: AN INCANTATION THAT WILL UNLOCK THE TRUE POWER OF THE PHILOSOPHER'S STONE. PRAETORIOUS HAS BOTH IN HIS POSSESSION NOW.
I'VE MANAGED TO RESTORE MICHAEL'S ORGAN AND ELECTRICAL IMPULSE FUNCTIONS, BUT THERE'S ONE MORE PROCEDURE I NEED TO PERFORM BEFORE I CAN SEW HIM BACK UP.
YOU SEE THIS METAL RING AROUND HIS HEART? THE ONE WITH THE STRANGE WRITING STAMPED INTO IT?
MICHAEL SAYS THE WRITING ON THAT RING IS A COUNTER-INCANTATION VICTOR FRANKENSTEIN PLACED IT THERE AS A FINAL DEFENSE AGAINST THE STONE. TROUBLE IS, WE CAN'T READ IT WITHOUT REMOVING IT.
IF YOU REMOVE IT... WHAT HAPPENS TO MICHAEL?
IT'S THE ONLY WAY.

"IF WE DON'T STOP PRAETORIOUS AND THAT HATEFUL WOMAN NOW, ALL OF GOD'S CHILDREN WILL SUFFER."
I FEEL IT, DOCTOR. THE STONE PULSES WITH VIBRANT LIFE AND RAW POWER...
...AND WE WILL USE THAT POWER TO RESHAPE THIS WASTED REALITY INTO A KINGDOM WORTHY OF ITS NEW RULERS.

ISSUE FOUR

From the journals of
Victor Frankenstein:
I can endure this damnable wait no longer.
My desire to possess the Philosopher's Stone has cost me dearly. I think perhaps I shall never know the secrets of the stone, and I must make peace with that.
My greatest creation lies before me; his glorious birth requires nothing more than the blessing of a neglectful creator.
"The stone shall be the heart" - I set that goal for myself. Though I failed in the pursuit, I have taken care to ensure that a reversal of fortune will not catch me unprepared.
There will be a place for all things; for every action, a well-devised reaction.
In this moment, however, there is only life.

"IT STARTED WITH DEATH. IT ALWAYS STARTS WITH DEATH FOR US, DOESN'T IT?
"THAT REPORTER IN PHILLY GOT HIS FUCKING BRAINS BLOWN OUT BECAUSE HE TRIED TO HELP US. SOMEONE HAD BEEN DIGGING UP SLASHERS THAT WE KILLED... BUT WHO? AND WHY?
"WE FOLLOWED THE TRAIL TO NEW YORK UNIVERSITY; THAT'S WHERE WE MET EVA. SHE NEEDED HELP FINDING HER FRIEND, WHO APPEARED TO HAVE BEEN KIDNAPPED BY THE SAME SON OF A BITCH WHO'D BEEN STEALING THE CORPSES OF OUR ENEMIES.
"NEXT THING YOU KNOW, WE'RE IN SOME SHITHOLE DETROIT SUBURB, FIGHTING WEREWOLVES AND WEIRDOS WITH EVA AND THE LOCAL TRIGGER-HAPPY COWBOY BRIGADE.
"BUT WHAT ABOUT OUR SLASHERS? SERGEANT KRAMER? EMILY CRISTY? LLOYD AND JIMMY? THE WAKING MAN? WE GOT INTO THIS WHOLE SHIT-UATION WITH THE INTENTION OF GETTING SOME ANSWERS ON THAT FRONT...
"...AND SOMEWHERE ALONG THE WAY, WE TOOK OUR EYES OFF THE FUCKING BALL."
DETROIT, MICHIGAN

WHEN DID THIS STOP BEING OUR STORY, VLAD?
WHY DO YOU CARE?
I DON'T KNOW. MAYBE THIS IS BIGGER THAN US. MAYBE FATE HAD OTHER PLANS.
HRRRN. FATE HAS NOTHING TO DO WITH IT, CASSIE.
OKAY, THEN. THAT'S FINE...
...BUT TAKING FATE OUT OF THE EQUATION JUST REINFORCES THE VERY BAD FEELING I HAVE IN MY GUTS. TRUST ME, THE OTHER SHOE'S GONNA DROP--
--WHAT THE SHIT?
HRRNN. LOOKS LIKE A WHOLE BUNCH OF SHOES ARE DROPPING.

IT'S TAKEN FIVE TIMES THE USUAL AMOUNT OF ANAESTHETIC TO EVEN MAKE YOU BLEARY-EYED, MICHAEL.
I'LL DO MY BEST TO MAKE THIS AS PAINLESS AS POSSIBLE.
IT'S TIME. I'LL LET YOU KNOW WHEN YOU CAN COME BACK IN.
I WON'T PRETEND I UNDERSTAND THE FIRST THING ABOUT THE WORK THAT'S GOING TO HAPPEN IN THAT ROOM, EVA...
...BUT I DO KNOW THAT TOM NORD IS A GREAT DOCTOR. YOUR FRIEND IS IN GOOD HANDS, AND I'M SURE HE'LL MAKE IT THROUGH THIS JUST FINE.
THANK YOU FOR THE REASSURANCE, SHEPHERD...
...BUT YOUR DOCTOR IS HELPING MICHAEL MAKE A SACRIFICE, NOT A RECOVERY.
WHAT? I'M SORRY... I HAD NO IDEA.
MOVE IT! HRRRNNN! SHITHEAD PARADE COMING OUR WAY!
YOU'RE TELLIN' ME--

MONSTERS AND UNDEAD SLASHERS INCOMING. THEY'RE MARCHING RIGHT UP TO THE FRONT DOOR.
COEY! EUGENE! MEET US IN THE LOBBY ASAP!
WHAT ABOUT MICHAEL? HE'S IN SURGERY--
WE'LL ALL BE IN SURGERY IF WE LOSE THIS FIGHT. COME ON.
COEY! SITREP.
I COUNT FOUR UNIQUE FREAKS AND ABOUT TWO DOZEN OF THOSE CRAZY-ASS PLAY-DOH PEOPLE.
IS IT WEIRD THAT I'M NOT EVEN FAZED BY THIS CRAP ANYMORE? HELL, WE RESCUED THE FRANKENSTEIN DUDE FROM A WOMAN WITH A STITCHED-UP FACE AND TENTACLES--
--WHAT DID YOU JUST SAY?!
WHY DIDN'T YOU TELL US ABOUT THE WOMAN, YOU DUMB MOTHERFUCKER?!
I'M SORRY, OKAY? I THOUGHT WE TOLD EVERYONE! WHO IS SHE, ANYWAY?
TELL THEM WHO I AM, CASSANDRA! TELL YOUR FRIENDS ALL ABOUT THE DAY YOU KILLED MARY SHELLEY LOVECRAFT!

TOO MANY REALITIES PASSING INTO MY VIEW AT ONCE;
MY CONNECTION WITH THE GIRL AND HER LOPING MANSERVANT HAS BEEN SEVERED.
IT'S NO MATTER. WE HAVE THE PHILOSOPHER'S STONE, AND THE INCANTATION THAT UNLOCKS ITS TRUE POWER. VICTOR FRANKENSTEIN WAS A FOOL TO THINK THAT HE COULD HIDE IT FOREVER.
HIS INTELLECT WAS NO MATCH FOR OUR COMBINED WISDOM, MY DARLING.
NEITHER SHALL THE WORLD BE, PRAETORIOUS.
THAT IS WHY I REACHED OUT ACROSS THE VAST CANYONS OF THOUGHT-REALITY TO JOIN OUR MINDS AND BODIES TOGETHER UPON THE SAME PLANE.
STAND WITH ME NOW, IN THE HOUR OF OUR KINGDOM COME.

BASTARDS! THEY'RE FIRING ON US!
SCURRY LIKE RATS IF YOU WANT...
BRAKA
AKA
AKA AKA AKA
...BUT I'M NOT SO EASILY SCARED.
SKRASH
HURRRRRNNN!
TIME TO DIE AGAIN.
TAKE HIM DOWN! DOUBLE-TIME, YOU MAGGOTS!
SHUUUK
HOLD YOUR FIRE. WAIT FOR A CLEAR SHOT.

SURPRISED TO SEE ME, WHORE?
GOD, I WISH--
AARRYUUUGH!
WE HAVE NO TIME TO SPARE FOR MERCY. YOU'VE BEEN WARNED.
OOOH, SCARY.
EVA, WATCH OUT-- OOF!-- FOR THE LITTLE FUCKER IN HIS CHEST!
RRRGRGGGH
TOO LATE!
DISGUSTING LITTLE CRETIN--
BLAM
SHPLUUUK

I'M IN YOUR DEBT, SHEPHERD.
NO SENSE IN TALLYING IT UP YET, EVA. KEEP FIGHTING.
JIMMY! WHAT DID YOU TO DO HIM?! JIIIMMMMYY!
JOIN HIM.
KSHOKKRAKK
HURRNGGH! KILL! YOU! ALL!
DON'T YOU WANT ME TO TOUCH YOU, CASSIE?
I BET YOU'D LOVE THE FEELING OF MY HANDS ON YOUR SOFT, SWEET SKIN!
I'D RATHER BE THE ONLY WOMAN IN A PORNO WITH HALF A DOZEN STEREOTYPE MINORITY WEREWOLVES, EMILY...
AND NOT JUST BECAUSE THAT'S SOMETHING I COULD EASILY ARRANGE IN THIS SHITHOLE TOWN.
BRAKAAKAKAAKA
DUCK AND COVER, CASSIE!

TRINITY MEDICAL CLINIC
"WHILE WE WERE SACRIFICING OUR SANITY TO THE BLOOD AND HEAT OF WAR...
"...MICHAEL TURNED THE TIDE OF BATTLE IN OUR FAVOR, BY SURRENDERING THE MOST PRECIOUS GIFT THAT ANY LIVING CREATURE CAN KNOW. HE HAS LED US TO GLORY, BUT HE WILL NEVER SEE US CLAIM IT."

THE RING WAS A BINDING OF HIS HEART; A SECRET DEFENSE AGAINST THE STONE.
AN INCANTATION OF REVERSAL. HIDDEN WITHIN LIFE, REVEALED ONLY BY DEATH...
...AND WRITTEN IN AN ANCIENT TONGUE, TAUGHT TO ME IN MY YOUTH BY THE MONKS WHO RAISED ME.
LONG STORY SHORT: EVA'S THE ONLY ONE WHO CAN READ THE SECRET CODE. VLAD AND I ARE GOING TO HELP HER PUT AN END TO THIS...
...BUT THE REST OF YOU SHOULD GET THE HELL OUT OF HERE A.S.P.C.A., COMPRENDE?
I THINK I SPEAK FOR EVERYONE WHEN I SAY "FUCK THAT NOISE." COMPRENDE?
YEAH, YOU SPEAK FOR *KOFF* EVERYONE.
WE'RE THE GHOSTS OF OLD DETROIT, CASSIE. THAT'S OUR GIG. WE STAY.
WHAT ARE YOU DOING UP AND AROUND, J.R.? YOU NEED TO REST.
ARE YOU MY *UNNNGH* BROTHER, OR MY MOMMY? I'M FINE. *KOFF* GUESS I WOULDN'T MIND LEANING INSTEAD OF STANDING, THOUGH...
OKAY, LOOKS LIKE WE'RE ALL IN. I'LL EXPLAIN THE SPECIFICS WHILE WE LOAD UP THE RIGS, BUT THE RING ISN'T THE ONLY SECRET WEAPON WE HAVE.
THIS JAGGED SPIKE ONCE SPILLED THE BLOOD OF MY SAVIOR. WHATEVER YOU CHOOSE TO BELIEVE, HAVE FAITH IN MY ACCOUNT: I HAVE SEEN IT BRING AN END TO BEINGS OF THE PUREST EVIL, AND I KNOW IT WILL AGAIN.
THEY'RE COMING, PRAETORIOUS...

"...AND THEY ARE COMING WITH THE SOLE INTENT OF ENDING US."
PRAETORIOUS! LOVECRAFT! LET IT BE KNOWN THAT YOUR LAST MOMENTS ARE UPON YOU! IF YOU BELIEVE YOURSELVES CAPABLE AND WORTHY OF SALVATION, YOU WOULD BE WISE TO TAKE A KNEE AND PRAY NOW!
THE STONE--!
WHAT'S HAPPENING TO IT?!
I...I DON'T KNOW! I'VE NEVER SEEN IT GLOW LIKE THAT BEFORE...
I CAN FEEL THE ENERGY, DOCTOR. IT'S RESONATING THROUGH THE DIMENSIONAL FABRIC...REVERSING EVERYTHING WE'VE DONE..!"

NOT FOR LONG, SWEET MARY.
LOOK AROUND US, YOU OVERBLOWN CHARLATAN! THE CHANGE IS ALREADY HAPPENING, AND SIMPLY REPEATING THE INCANTATION ISN'T GOING TO HAVE ANY EFFECT NOW!
YOUR THINKING IS ONE-DIMENSIONAL. YOU DON'T APPRECIATE THE MULTITUDE OF ASPECTS I CAN DRAW FROM THE NARROW SPACES BETWEEN REALITIES...
AND MERGE INTO THIS DIMENSION, CREATING A PATCHWORK PRESENT THAT CAN BE STITCHED TOGETHER AS A MOSAIC OF FINALITY-- NO!
BWOMWOMWOMWOMWOM
BWOM
THIS CAN'T HAPPEN! IT DOESN'T WORK LIKE THIS!
BWOM
BWOMWOMWOM
IT'S PUNCHING ITS WAY THROUGH A DOZEN DIFFERENT REALITIES AND RETURNING HERE! THE BOUNDARIES ASSUMED BY THE ARCANE MATH LAWS ARE BEING FORCED INTO OBSOLESCENCE. CAN'T YOU SEE IT?!
I CAN'T... I...JUST DON'T MOVE! I'M COMING!
BWOM
BWOMWOM
BWOOOOM

UUUAAAGH!
BWAZOM
IT'S CORRECTING YOUR HUMAN CONTINUITY, DOCTOR... ACCELERATING YOU TO YOUR PROPER AGE...
...AND ITS POWER IS GLORIOUS.

I HAVE SEEN THE END OF THIS REALITY AND THE BEGINNING OF A THOUSAND MORE. I AM NOT CONFINED BY IGNORANCE, AND I WILL NOT BE IMPRISONED BY THE RESTRICTIONS OF THIS REALITY'S PHYSICAL LAWS.
IF I CANNOT ESCAPE WITHOUT...
BAAAA
WHAAAHOM
YES! YES! ALL OF THE ENERGY! ALL OF THE POWER! FEED ME!
FEEEEEED MEEEEEEEE!

KNOCK HRRRRN KNOCK!
THEY'RE IN! THEY'RE IN! PUSH THE BUTTON!
PUSH THE FUCKING BUTTON RIGHT NOW!
YOU WANNA BE FED, YOU SUPER-SIZED SNATCH?!
'CAUSE YOU CAN EAT ME ALL DAY LONG!
KA BOO OOM

KRAKOOOOOM
HNNNNGH!
EEEYYYAAAAAAAH
OOF!
WHOOMP

I DREW YOU IN. I MADE YOU FACE THE DEAD AGAIN, MADE YOU UNDERSTAND THAT DEATH IS NOT FINAL...IT'S NEVER FINAL...
YOU WILL NOT KILL ME NOT KILL ME
TECHNICALLY, IT'S "YOU WILL NOT KILL ME AGAIN." DID YOU FORGET THAT WE'VE ALREADY DONE THAT DANCE?
DOESN'T MATTER, REALLY. FOR WHAT IT'S WORTH, YOU'RE ABSOLUTELY RIGHT: WE'RE NOT GOING TO KILL YOU...
...'CAUSE WE FIGURED IT WAS ONLY FAIR TO LET EVA HAVE A TURN.
EEEYYYAAAAAAH
SKRAAAAAK
KSHUUK

NONONO NONONO NOUUUUAAAAH
HUH. ONLY A WOMAN STILL TALKS AFTER GETTING HER HEAD CUT OFF. HEH-HEH-HEH.
HOO-BOY. MAKE SURE AND PUT THAT ONE IN YOUR COMEDY ROUTINE, SEINFELD. FUCKIN' HILARIOUS.
NONONNNNN--
KSHPLUUK
OH, I SEE HOW IT IS. SWEET-MEAT AND I HAVE TO CHUCK ALL THE SHITTY, BLOODY PARTS INTO THE DIMENSIONAL PORTALS WHILE YOU STAND BY WIPING YOUR SPIKE.
YOU THINK THAT'S ROUGH WORK?
I HAD TO REACH ALL THE WAY DOWN TO THE GROUND TO PICK UP THE MAGIC FRISBEE. JESUS, I'M EXHAUSTED...
...AND I JUST KNOW THAT THE ASSHOLES IN THE FUNNY COSTUMES ARE GONNA GET ALL THE CREDIT FOR THIS ONE.

"The stone shall be the heart."
Sh-chok
IS HE...?
JUST WAIT. LET'S SEE WHAT HAPPENS.
MICHAEL?
MICHAEL, YOU'RE ALL RIGHT. YOU'RE ALIVE..!
MASTER.
WHERE. MASTER?

HE DOES NOT...
...HE DOES NOT REMEMBER ANYTHING. HE DOES NOT REMEMBER ME. MICHAEL, DO YOU REMEMBER? REMEMBER EVA?
EVA, I'M SORRY.
REMEMBER...
...MASTER.
YEAH, I KNOW WE NEED TO GET TO A REAL HOSPITAL. JUST GIVE ME A SECOND.
I'VE GOT THIS. YOU REST.
THANK YOU FOR EVERYTHING. I HOPE YOU'LL COME AND VISIT UNDER BETTER CIRCUMSTANCES.
WE'LL SEE. NOT MANY VACATIONS IN OUR LINE OF WORK, Y'KNOW.
THANKS TO YOU AS WELL, EVA. WE'RE ALL VERY SORRY FOR YOUR LOSS...
...BUT I HOPE YOU KNOW THAT YOU NEVER HAVE TO BE ALONE.
YOU'RE WELCOME TO STAY HERE AND JOIN OUR TEAM, IF YOU'D LIKE.

I'VE NEVER MET ANYONE LIKE YOU. I HOPE WE SEE EACH OTHER AGAIN SOMEDAY.
IF GOD WILLS IT...WELL, IF GOD WILLS IT FOR ME.
I HOPE HE DOES.
YOU'RE SURE YOU'D RATHER STAY HERE?
FOR NOW.
TO SEE YOU BOTH SMILING AND NOT STABBING...
...IT MAKES ME THINK THAT SOMETHING BETTER IS HAPPENING HERE TODAY.
CASSIE, I WANT TO KNOW. DO YOU THINK YOU COULD EVER HRRRNN HAVE THAT KIND OF FAITH?
HAVING FAITH IS JUST ANOTHER WAY TO SURVIVE. FAITH IS A GUN, OR A KNIFE. TRUE LOVE, OR TRUE HATE. IT'S SOMETHING TO BELIEVE IN.
MY FAITH WILL NEVER BE THE SAME AS HERS, BUT THAT DOESN'T MEAN A GODDAMN THING IN THIS WORLD.
I BELIEVE IN SURVIVING. YOU DO WHAT YOU HAVE TO DO, AND YOU KEEP ON LIVING. AMEN.
THE END

COVER GALLERY
BY TIM SEELEY

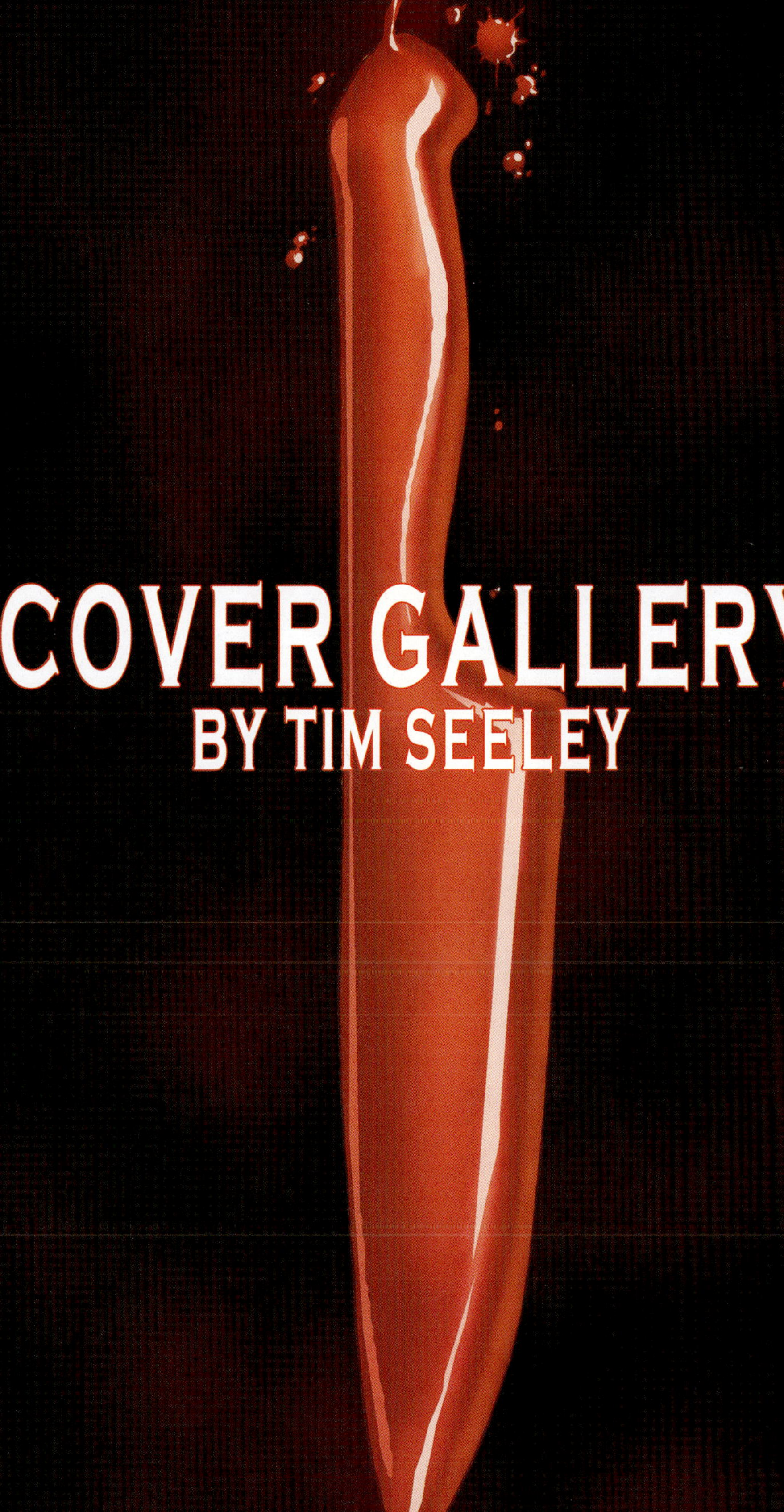